THE ARABIAN NIGHTS
CHILDREN'S COLLECTION

Dados Internacionais de Catalogação na Publicação (CIP) de acordo com ISBD

J76a   Jones, Kellie
          Aladdin and the magic lamp / adaptado por Kellie Jones. – Jandira : W. Books, 2025.
          128 p. ; 12,8cm x 19,8cm. – (The Arabian nights)

          ISBN: 978-65-5294-177-0

          1. Literatura infantojuvenil. 2. Contos. 3. Contos de Fadas. 4. Literatura Infantil.
          5. Clássicos. 6. Mágica. 7. Histórias. I. Título. II. Série.

2025-600   CDD 028.5
                                          CDU 82-93

Elaborado por Vagner Rodolfo da Silva - CRB-8/9410
Índice para catálogo sistemático:
1. Literatura infantojuvenil 028.5
2. Literatura infantojuvenil 82-93

The Arabian Nights 10 Book Collection
Text © Sweet Cherry Publishing Limited, 2023
Inside illustrations © Sweet Cherry Publishing Limited, 2023
Cover illustrations © Sweet Cherry Publishing Limited, 2023

Text based on translations of the original folk tale,
adapted by Kellie Jones
Illustrations by Grace Westwood

© 2025 edition:
Ciranda Cultural Editora e Distribuidora Ltda.

1st edition in 2025
www.cirandacultural.com.br
No part of this publication may be reproduced, stored in a retrieval
system, or transmitted in any form or by any means, electronic,
mechanical, photocopying, recording, or otherwise, without written
permission of the publisher.
This book is a work of fiction. Names, characters, places, and incidents
are either the product of the author's imagination or are used fictitiously,
and any resemblance to actual persons, living or dead, business
establishments, events, or locales is entirely coincidental.

Long ago, in the ancient lands of Arabia, there lived a brave woman called Scheherazade. When the country's sultan went mad, Scheherazade used her cleverness and creativity to save many lives – including her own. She did this over a thousand and one nights, by telling the sultan stories of adventure, danger and enchantment.

This is just one of them …

Aladdin
The son of tailors

Mustapha
Aladdin's father

Ching
Aladdin's mother

Ja'far
A sorcerer

The Genies
*The genie of the ring &
the genie of the lamp*

The Emperor
The ruler of China

Princess Yue
The emperor's daughter

The Grand-Vizier
The emperor's advisor

The Grand-Vizier's Son
A potential husband for Princess Yue

Chapter 1

In a rich province of China where paper lanterns glowed, there lived a poor couple named Mustapha and Ching who had a son named Aladdin. While his parents worked hard to feed their family, Aladdin played on the crowded dirt streets and occasionally even the tiled rooftops around their home. He grew up wild and lazy, and ignored all efforts to change his ways.

When the time came for Aladdin to join his parents' trade as a tailor, he refused to learn one end of a needle from the other. No promises of reward or threats of punishment could change him. And even when Mustapha died and Ching was left alone to support them, Aladdin did not mend his ways – nor any clothing.

Instead, Aladdin continued to play with the other idle boys outside their dark, rickety wooden houses. There, one day, a stranger asked Aladdin his age, and if

tailor
Someone who makes, repairs or alters clothing to make it fit.

he was the son of Mustapha the tailor.

'I am, sir,' replied Aladdin, 'but he died a while ago. Now it is just me and my mother.'

At this the stranger hugged and kissed Aladdin, saying: 'I am your

uncle, and you look just like my brother. Go to your mother and tell her I am coming.'

Aladdin ran home and told his mother about his newfound uncle.

'It is true,' Ching said, 'your father did have a brother. But I thought he had died before your father and I met.'

Still, Ching prepared dinner with what little they had. But when she told Aladdin to fetch his uncle, the man came laden with food and drink. He kissed the place at their low table where

Mustapha used to sit, and he explained to Ching why they had never had the chance to meet. It was because he had been abroad for years.

'Abroad where?' Aladdin asked.

'Everywhere!' replied the man. 'You cannot name a place I have not been! But I spent most of my time in Africa.'

In fact, the man was from the Maghreb region in North Africa. But he did not say this. To do so would be admitting that he was no more related to the late Mustapha – who had come from India – than to any other person in China.

Over dinner, the man told stories of his travels that held even Aladdin's short attention. At fifteen years old,

the boy had barely gone beyond the streets where he played. Now he began to wonder about the world at large, and his place in it.

Eventually, the man turned to Aladdin and asked what he did for a living. At this question, the boy hung his head in shame. His mother, meanwhile, burst into tears.

'Nothing!' she wept. 'He does nothing but play with his friends! I am at my wits' end!'

Hearing that Aladdin was too lazy to learn a trade, the man offered to rent a shop for him and stock it with goods to sell. 'That way half the work will be done!' the man laughed. 'And perhaps you will enjoy life as a merchant more than life as a tailor.'

All Aladdin knew was that merchants were often rich, so he agreed.

'But first,' the man urged, 'let us spend some time and get to know each other.'

The next day, the man bought Aladdin a fine set of clothes and took him all over the city, touring sights from the finest mosques to

merchant
Someone who buys and sells goods.

the grandest inns. At nightfall,
he returned Aladdin to his
mother, who was delighted to
see her son looking so fine and
respectable.

By the next day, Aladdin was
well used to calling the man
'uncle', and together they went
to some beautiful gardens
a long way outside
the city gates.

There they sat down by a fountain, and the man pulled a cake from his bag, which he divided between them. Afterwards they journeyed on, past rice paddies and farmers in straw hats, then past water buffalo who stopped grazing to watch them. Finally they reached the mountains. By then, Aladdin was so tired that he begged to return home. But the man told him more stories of his travels. He convinced Aladdin to continue, despite the boy's tired legs.

rice paddy
A flooded field where rice is grown.

At last, they came to a narrow valley between two mountains.

'We go no further,' said the man. 'Gather some sticks while I kindle a fire. Then I will show you something wonderful.'

Tired but excited, Aladdin did as he was told with more speed than he would usually give any task. When the fire was lit, the man, who was really a sorcerer named Ja'far and not Aladdin's uncle, threw on it a powder he carried with him. At the same

sorcerer
A man who claims or is believed to have magic powers.

time, he said some magic words. At these words, the earth began to shake. Soon it opened in front of them, revealing a flat, square stone with a brass ring in the middle to raise it by. Aladdin, who had been watching wide-eyed in shock, tried to run away. But Ja'far caught him.

'What is this magic, uncle?'
Aladdin cried. 'Let me go!'

Ja'far replied, 'Do as I say, boy,
and you will have nothing to fear.

Beneath this stone lies a treasure only you can reach. But you must do exactly as I tell you.'

At the word "treasure", Aladdin forgot his fears. He reached for the ring in the middle of the stone square and looked at Ja'far expectantly. 'Are you not going to help me?'

'I cannot.' Ja'far shook his head. 'That is why I need you.'

When Ja'far told him to grasp the ring and lift the stone, Aladdin grasped and lifted obediently. The heavy stone came up surprisingly – even magically

– easily. Beneath it were steps that led into complete darkness. Aladdin shivered.

'At the foot of the steps,' Ja'far told him, 'you will find an open door leading into three large halls. Pass through them without touching anything, or you will die instantly. The halls lead into a garden of fine fruit trees. Walk on until you come to a terrace – and there stands a lighted lamp. Put out the lamp, pour out the oil and bring it to me.'

'A lamp?' Aladdin echoed, his obedience waning. 'You want me to go down there for *a lamp*? My own mother has one of those. You can have it.'

The sorcerer gritted his teeth. 'But I want *this* lamp.'

'You said there was treasure down there.'

'There is.'

'But I cannot touch any of it?'

'You can touch the fruit.'

'The fruit?' Aladdin repeated. 'You want me to risk my life for an oil lamp and some fruit?'

'You will not die so long as you follow my instructions.'

'How do you know?'

With a sigh, Ja'far drew a ring from his finger and gave it to Aladdin. 'Wear this,' he said, '*and* follow my instructions. Then you will be protected from harm.'

Aladdin accepted the talisman and trudged slowly underground. There, instead of mud caves, he found smooth, polished rooms carved from stone.

Everything was as the sorcerer had said, and Aladdin did everything as he had been told. The three great halls contained more money than he had ever imagined – gleaming coins piled up in mountains along the walls. The first hall held brass, the second silver, the third gold.

talisman
An object, often worn or carried, that is believed to protect the owner or have special powers.

In each, a rainbow of jewels winked at him as he passed, reflecting the dim light that came from somewhere unseen.

Aladdin's eyes were wide and his mouth was dry as he saw all of this, but he did not touch any of it. Then he reached the underground orchard, which glittered even more than the jewels had. The fruit was so strange that he did not dare to eat it, but so beautiful that he could not resist stuffing some into his pockets, purse and even his tunic. The load grew quite heavy.

On the terrace, Aladdin stopped to warm his hands a little before extinguishing the lamp. Finally, he returned to the mouth of the cave, where the sorcerer waited impatiently.

'Hurry and give me the lamp!' he said, before Aladdin had even reached the top of the steps.

'Wait until I am out,' said Aladdin. By now he was tired of doing what he was told. He spoke with a stubbornness that his mother was used to, but Ja'far was not.

'Give me the lamp!' Ja'far shouted angrily.

'Just wait!' Aladdin shouted back. He was angry, too, and weighed down by the strange, glassy fruit from the underground orchard.

Hearing this refusal, and seeing that Aladdin was moving very slowly yet not knowing the cause, Ja'far flew into a rage. He threw more powder onto the fire, muttered more magic words and again the earth shook. Where before the stone slab had slid open, this time, as Aladdin watched, it slid shut.

When it did not open again, Aladdin concluded, quite rightly: 'I do not believe that man was my uncle after all ...'

Chapter 2

Ja'far soon regretted his show of temper. He found himself separated from the lamp that would have made him the most powerful man in the world. A prophecy had told him that he would have only one chance to get it, and that he could choose only one person to fetch it for him. Seeing Aladdin playing

prophecy
An act of seeing into the future to predict or warn of future events.

in the streets that day, so lazy and lacking in ambition of his own, Ja'far had chosen him and intended to kill him after gaining the lamp. But oh, how he regretted that now.

And how Aladdin regretted agreeing to search for it.

Indeed, as time passed in the gloom underground, Aladdin had time to regret many things.

'Forgive me, mother,' he wept at the end of the first full day. 'Your worthless son has brought you nothing but disappointment. Now you will not even know what became of him.'

'Father,' he sobbed on the second day, 'I fear I will follow you in death soon.'

But on the third day, as he alternated between wringing his hands with worry and clasping them in prayer, Aladdin happened to rub the ring that Ja'far had given him.

Immediately, a huge and terrifying genie appeared.

'Greetings, master,' the genie boomed. 'I am the genie of the ring, and I will grant you three wishes.'

'Get me out of here!' Aladdin cried, too fearful already to fear any more.

'Your wish is my command.'

In the blink of an eye, Aladdin found himself above ground again, where he fell to his knees on the ground and kissed it. He had half expected to find the sorcerer waiting for him. But Ja'far had left in the belief that Aladdin must be dead.

Having run out of water the day before, Aladdin's second wish was to go to the fountain where he had stopped with the sorcerer. There he drank until his empty belly cramped. He had already tried to eat the strange, glassy fruit from the underground orchard. Having nearly broken his teeth in the attempt, he had left it behind rather than spend his energy carrying it.

Daylight stung his eyes, but it was fading when he reached home and fainted on the doorstep.

'Aladdin!' Ching cried when she answered the door to find him lying there. 'What happened? Where is your uncle?'

Wearily, Aladdin told his mother what had passed with the sorcerer. When he finished, he asked, 'Is there anything to eat? I am starving.'

'There is nothing, but I have spun some cotton. I will go and sell it to buy food.'

But Aladdin, who had grown up a bit after his experience of the past few days, held up the lamp and stopped her. 'Keep your cotton, mother. It is my turn to put food on the table. I will go and sell this.'

'Let me clean it first,' said Ching.

The lamp was dull with dust and black with soot. As Ching polished it with a piece of cloth, another genie appeared.

'Greetings, master,' the second genie boomed. 'I am the genie of the lamp, and I will grant you *unlimited* wishes.'

'Bring me something to eat!' Aladdin said boldly.

'Your wish is my command.'

In the blink of an eye, their small wooden table overflowed with silver bowls, cups and plates, all bearing rich meats such as chicken, duck, goose and pork, and vegetables such as yams, beans and turnips. The air was flavoured with the scent of spring onions and garlic. It was warmed by clouds of steam from newly uncovered baskets of rice, noodles and dumplings.

Ching gaped in surprise as Aladdin dug in.

'Eat,' said Aladdin, although it sounded like 'Eeb' with his mouth full.

'But where did it all come from?' Ching asked as she sat beside her son.

"'agic,' said Aladdin – meaning 'magic'.

The pair dined into the night, although at first the food did not sit well with Ching. She still remembered the fearsome genie who had summoned it.

'Tomorrow you should sell the lamp,' she told Aladdin. 'And the ring.'

'Tomorrow I will wish for more food!' Aladdin corrected her. 'You have nothing to fear. Between the genie of the ring and the lamp, our troubles are over.'

The next day, rather than the lamp or the ring, Aladdin sold one of the silver plates. Then he sold another and another and another, until none were left. Then he called upon the genie of the lamp for more and sold those. And so they lived comfortably for years, with enough food to share with those who were still as poor as they had once been.

One day, there was an order from the Emperor of China. All the people in Aladdin's province were told to stay home and shutter their windows while the emperor's daughter, Princess Yue, passed through.

Aladdin was now an adult, and a better son. He had found success as a merchant after all, even if he was one who only sold silver tableware. But after the incident with the sorcerer Ja'far, Aladdin

emperor
The male ruler of an empire.

hated following orders more than ever.

When Princess Yue rode by his house, which was now much larger and on a richer street in the province, Aladdin looked through a gap in the shutters. He expected to see only a palanquin carried by royal guards, with the princess hidden away inside it. But although there was such a carriage, Princess Yue walked beside it and looked all around her, curious about how her father's people lived. As the breeze lifted

palanquin
A seat or box used as transport, carried by poles on the shoulders of several people.

the princess's veil, Aladdin saw her very well indeed. Her face was like a full moon, and her hair was like the night sky surrounding it.

Aladdin fell in love at first sight. 'I am going to marry Princess Yue,' he said as he stepped away from the window.

His mother, overhearing this, could only laugh.

'You? Marry a princess? Ha!'

'I mean it, mother. I have never wanted anything more.'

In fact, Aladdin had never wanted anything at all. This was the root of his laziness: he simply did not want anything enough to work for it. Until now.

'You must go to the emperor and ask him to give me his daughter's hand in marriage.'

'Me?' Ching said. 'Go to the emperor?'

'Who else?' Aladdin replied.

'Please, mother. Only yesterday you were telling me it was time for me to marry.'

'I was thinking of a merchant's daughter!'

'It is Princess Yue or no one,' Aladdin vowed.

So the next day Ching went to the palace to speak to the Emperor of China. She carried with her a special gift.

When Aladdin had stood up after the first meal the genie of the lamp had magicked for him, Ching had pointed to a lump in his clothing. She joked that he was getting fat already, but the bulge turned out to be his harvest from the underground orchard. Though Aladdin had emptied his pockets and purse back at the cave, he had forgotten to empty his tunic.

Wrapped in a silk scarf woven
by his mother were the inedible
gemfruits. The lemons were yellow
diamonds, the apples were jade
and ruby, and the lone persimmon
was made of an orange topaz
the size of a fist. Smaller but no
less beautiful were the garnet
cherries, pearl apricots and
sapphire figs. There
was even an emerald
leaf Aladdin did
not remember
picking. It was a
gift worthy of
an emperor.

But in the great hall full of red pillars where the emperor received his visitors, Ching was one of many people trying to get his attention. She did not succeed the first day, but Aladdin begged her not to give up. She went every day for a week and stood in the same spot. At the end of the week, the emperor said to his grand-vizier, 'There is a woman who comes here every day carrying something in

grand-vizier
Someone like a modern-day prime minister. They did not just advise royal families in the old Turkish empire and in Islamic countries, they represented them and led the government. More powerful than a vizier.

a scarf. If she comes tomorrow, summon her to speak.'

The next day, Ching was called to the foot of the throne, which sat at the top of a small staircase. There she knelt and bowed.

'Rise, good woman,' the emperor said, 'and tell me what you want.'

Ching hesitated. 'Your Majesty, my son is in love with your daughter, Princess Yue. He begged me to come here to ask you to grant him her hand in marriage, but I know it is impossible. I hope you will forgive us both for our boldness.

I do not wish to waste your time.'

Fortunately, the emperor was more amused than insulted. Ching looked respectable and spoke well, but it was clear

to him that her son could not
be the equal of his daughter, a
princess. He agreed that it was
impossible for the two of them
to marry.

'But I am curious,' the
emperor said, before Ching
could back away. 'What is it
that you carry with you?'

Ching passed the scarf to the
grand-vizier, who unfolded it
and presented the gemfruits
to the emperor. The emperor
gasped and looked at Ching
with fresh eyes. She must be
from a very rich family after all!

To the grand-vizier he whispered, 'What should I do? A man who would give this treasure for my daughter must love her greatly indeed.'

The grand-vizier, who wanted Princess Yue to marry his own son, advised the emperor to wait three months to decide. The emperor agreed to this and told Aladdin's mother that he would think about her request. He asked her not to appear before him again for three months while he did.

Ching expected Aladdin to be disappointed, but he was not.

He waited patiently and excitedly for two months, until Ching went to the market late one morning and found everyone there celebrating.

'What has happened?' she asked a nearby woman.

'Princess Yue is getting married!'

Ching was shocked. 'Getting married to whom?'

'The grand-vizier's son!'

Chapter 3

The grand-vizier had used the past two months to prepare an even greater offering for the emperor than the gemfruits. Now it was his son who was going to marry the princess.

Ching ran and told the news to Aladdin, who was shocked at first too. Then he thought of the lamp and rubbed it.

'Greetings, master,' the genie

said as he appeared. 'How may I serve you?'

'Genie, Princess Yue is going to marry another man.'

'I know, master, as I know all things.'

'Does the princess love him?'

'No, master. He is attempting to win her heart even now.'

'Bring them to me.'

'Your wish is my command.'

In the blink of an eye, a very surprised princess and grand-vizier's son appeared in Aladdin's home. They had been drinking tea together in the palace courtyard and they appeared with the inlaid

table and tray still between them.

'What is this magic?' the grand-vizier's son demanded, jumping to his feet. 'Who are you?'

'I am Princess Yue's future husband.'

The grand-vizier's son laughed in Aladdin's face. 'And I am her current one.'

'You are not married yet.'

'As good as! The wedding will take place in a month.'

'Yes,' Aladdin agreed, 'but it will be *my* wedding.'

While the men argued, the princess did not waste time wondering how she had left the palace. Whatever the magic, she was grateful for it, because it would have been much more difficult for her to leave by herself.

'I do not plan to marry either of you,' she said. 'I plan to run away.'

'But my father has already paid the wedding price!' the grand-vizier's son objected.

'I refuse to be bought!' snapped Princess Yue. 'I do not care what gifts anyone offers my father. I will choose my own husband.'

The grand-vizier's son scoffed. 'Nonsense!'

But Aladdin agreed with the princess. After all, he did not like being told what to do either.

'Why is that nonsense?' he asked the grand-vizier's son.

'Would you not like to choose your own wife?'

'I do not want a wife at all! I want to have fun! My father hardly lets me leave the palace. All I do is study.'

'Then let me go,' said Princess Yue, 'and we will both be happier.'

'What about me?' asked Aladdin. 'I will not be happier – I am in love with you.'

Now it was Princess Yue's turn to scoff. 'You do not even know me! If you did, I am sure your love would fade.

'And if you knew *me*,' Aladdin

returned, 'I am sure your love would grow.'

'You are very confident!'

Aladdin grinned – and for the first time the princess saw what a nice smile it was. The face around it was pleasing, too. She looked

about her and saw that the house
they were in was not large, but
it was richly furnished (thanks
to the genie of the lamp). *Is he a
nobleman?* Princess Yue wondered
of Aladdin.

Then she shrugged and said: 'It
makes no difference. We will never
know who is right.'

The grand-vizier's son interrupted.
'Princess, you cannot run from
the palace. My father will find
you, and the emperor will be
very upset.'

Princess Yue sighed. This was
true. Her father loved her best

of all his children. He would not have been persuaded to marry her away for just gold and jewels. The grand-vizier must have convinced him that his son would make her happy. It was for that reason that they were supposed to drink tea together every day at noon until the wedding. The emperor wanted them to get to know each other. After which, he fully expected Princess Yue to fall in love with her future husband, who was both handsome and clever.

He used some of that cleverness now. 'What if …' the grand-vizier's son began, thinking out loud. 'What if, instead of drinking tea together every day, we come here instead?'

'Yes!' said Aladdin, who was ready to agree to anything to spend more time with the princess.

'For what reason?' Princess Yue asked.

'Fun. *Freedom*,' said the grand-vizier's son. 'At least for a month, for an hour a day, we can do as we wish.'

'And after a month?'

'Then you can tell the emperor that you have tried but you do not love me.'

'Or that you are in love with someone else,' Aladdin suggested, meaning himself.

'Oh, very well,' the princess agreed. 'We will come here every day for a month, but only so that I can think of what to do at the end of it. If I am going to run away, it would be better to make a plan and gather supplies first.'

She had no faith at all that she would fall in love with Aladdin, so at first Princess Yue spent more time with his mother, who still lived with him. Ching liked to keep busy, and while she no longer needed to make clothes, she still enjoyed it. She made Princess Yue something more comfortable

and less noticeable
to wear outside of
the palace. The
princess, in
return, shared
her embroidery skills
with Ching, who could not believe
the beauty of her work.

Aladdin was happy to see the
two people he cared most about
getting along so well together, but
he was anxious that the princess
should get along with *him* too.

'Princess Yue, now that you
have plain clothes and might walk
outside without being recognised,

shall we go somewhere together?'
Aladdin suggested one day.

Princess Yue looked out of the
window at where she longed to
explore freely.

'All right,' she agreed. 'I want to
see how my father's people live.'

'Do you really?' Aladdin asked.

'Yes, of course.'

'Then I know just the place.'

Princess Yue expected that place
to be the market, or somewhere
else where people gathered. She
was surprised when Aladdin led
her along narrowing streets, from
paving stones onto mud, and past

increasingly dirty houses. He greeted the people who lived there by name. People who looked poor and hungry. And she was even more surprised that these people greeted Aladdin in return, and seemed to know and like him.

She realised that Aladdin had changed his clothes before they left, dressing simply and plainly like her. He had also filled the bag he carried with food. Aladdin unpacked the bag and shared with the people who suddenly surrounded them. Princess Yue was frightened at first. All her life she had lived in the palace, with only short trips outside to visit the local baths or temples. She had always been guarded, and passed through areas where people lived comfortably and ate well. Even the servants at the palace did not go hungry. But these people looked hungry and desperate.

'They are just people like you and me,' Aladdin told her. 'Give them this,' and he handed her some bread.

Princess Yue tore off a hunk of bread. Immediately, the people crowded closer and she shrank back. She looked to Aladdin, expecting him to act like one of her guards and protect her. But he only nodded encouragingly.

Princess Yue cleared her throat. 'Could … could you all line up, please? I want to make sure everyone gets some food.'

The people did as she asked. Some even kissed her hand. When the bread was gone, Aladdin produced a bag of rice, which the princess scooped into their waiting hands. When that was gone, it was time to leave. The hour that she was meant to have spent drinking tea with the grand-vizier's son was over.

Princess Yue and Aladdin started back to the house. During the walk, she talked seriously about what she had experienced.

'My father cannot be aware of this suffering. If he did, he would help these people.'

'Perhaps,' Aladdin said, 'but you cannot tell him yourself or he will know what you have been doing.'

They reached Aladdin's house, and the grand-vizier's son had returned too. Every day, sometimes with the help of one of Aladdin's wishes, he went on his own adventures. Today, like yesterday, he had been watching horse-racing.

'Did you have fun?' Aladdin asked him.

The grand-vizier's son only smiled. Then he and the princess were transported back to the palace, where no one even knew they had left.

This went on for weeks. Despite himself, the grand-vizier's son came to think of Aladdin as a friend. The princess came to think of him as something more.

Together they often went to give food to people who needed it. Aladdin's smile, which the princess thought so lovely, was always on full display in these moments. In fact, he seemed even more comfortable among those people than he did among the merchants of the market, who seemed to know him just as well.

At the end of the month, they were walking home in a comfortable silence. The princess

walked slowly, reluctant to return to the palace. In her hands she carried flowers, and a pretty stone given to her in exchange for the food. In her hair was a hand-carved wooden comb given to her by a boy and his sister the week before. It had replaced the expensive ivory decorations from the palace.

Aladdin was even less eager for the princess to leave, so he led them down a route Princess Yue had not walked before.

ivory
A hard, off-white material that forms the tusks and teeth of elephants and other animals.

It would take a few minutes longer but bring them to the exact same place.

'You seem to know every street, rich or poor, like the back of your hand!' Princess Yue observed.

Aladdin wanted to tell her that these were the very streets he had played on as a child, and the same poor people he had played *with*. But he bit his tongue. What would happen once the princess knew about his low birth?

Princess Yue sighed when he did not answer her.

'You promised that if I knew you better I would love you more,' she said. 'But you are still a mystery. I do not even know by what magic you bring me here each day. Are you a sorcerer?'

Aladdin laughed and plucked a flower from her hand. Tucking it behind her ear, he asked, 'Can you love me whatever I am?'

'Yes,' she said. 'Unless you love me less now that you know me better?'

'No.' Aladdin shook his head. 'The opposite. Which means,' he added mischievously, 'that I was right and you were wrong.'

Princess Yue folded her arms and pretended to be cross. 'Oh, does it?'

'*And*,' he said, 'far more importantly, it means that I can ask the emperor for your hand in marriage.'

'Yes,' Princess Yue agreed. 'You can.'

Chapter 4

So Ching went once more to the palace and stood before the emperor. She reminded him that three months had passed. Then she offered the same gemfruits in exchange for Princess Yue's hand in marriage to her son.

The grand-vizier was in a foul mood. His son had announced that morning that he would not marry. Instead, he wanted to travel the country and neighbouring lands to find the best horses. After that, he wanted to breed them for racing. He was so excited by this plan that his father could neither persuade nor threaten him to abandon it.

Princess Yue, meanwhile, wasted no time reassuring the emperor that far from being disappointed by this, she was happy.

'I am not in love with the grand-vizier's son, anyway,' she said.

The emperor had been most surprised. 'But you seem so happy lately! Indeed, you have seemed happy and in love since the two of you started drinking tea together.'

To which the princess smiled secretively and repeated: 'I am not in love with the grand-vizier's son, father.'

Now the emperor looked at the rare, glittering gemfruits and thought that perhaps things had worked out for the best after all. But the grand-vizier sneered at the gift, and at Ching herself.

'Neither her son nor his offering seem worthy of your daughter, Your Majesty. I would ask for something more. Something that proves that he is not a commoner with stolen jewels. Something that proves that his love for Princess Yue is deep and true.'

'Very well.' The emperor turned to Ching. 'Bring me forty times my daughter's weight in gold and forty times her weight in jewels. Let these be carried by ...' He stopped and thought for a moment. 'Let these be carried by forty elephants and forty monkeys. If they appear before me within the next forty days, your son will marry my daughter by the fortieth night.'

Ching, like the emperor, thought that this was an impossible request. She hurried home to tell Aladdin. When she had finished, she said, 'You could not come by such a fortune in forty years, never mind forty days!'

But Aladdin replied, 'Really?
For Princess Yue, I will do this and
more within forty *minutes*.'

With that, Aladdin summoned
the genie of the lamp and sent his
mother back to the palace with
forty elephants (rare white ones
from Thailand) and forty monkeys
(trained and dressed in human
clothing). The elephants carried
forty lots of gold and jewels, while
the monkeys juggled gemfruits of
forty different kinds. There were
not just apples, apricots, cherries,
figs, lemons and persimmons,
but peaches and pears, dates and

dragonfruits. There were lychees like opals and grapefruits like citrine. There were more fruits than the people in the emperor's great hall – or the emperor himself – could recognise.

Even the grand-vizier was impressed. At the emperor's request, he caught a magical mangosteen as it flew through the air and passed it to him. It glowed like the darkest amethyst in the emperor's hand, and the emperor's mind was made up.

'Tell your son that he may indeed marry my daughter. Bring

him to the palace and I will welcome him with open arms.'

When Ching told Aladdin this, Aladdin looked down at his clothes. They were far better than he had worn as a child of the streets but not good enough for the future husband of Princess Yue.

Aladdin summoned the genie of the lamp.

'Genie, I want a scented bath, fine clothing and a horse more magnificent than any in the emperor's stable. My mother must travel in the most beautiful palanquin, attended by twenty servants bearing purses full of gold.'

It was no sooner said than done. As he passed through the streets, people who had played with Aladdin the child came to marvel at Aladdin the man. And Aladdin ordered the servants to be generous with the gold they carried. Soon the watcher's hands were full and the ground glittered.

At the palace the emperor came down from his throne and embraced Aladdin. He led him into a hall where a feast was spread, ready for Aladdin to marry the princess that very day.

Princess Yue was delighted, but the grand-vizier was not.

'Where is the princess to live?' he demanded. 'In a common merchant's house? She belongs in a palace!'

'He's right,' Aladdin replied, surprising everyone. 'I cannot marry you, Yue.' At the princess's gasp, he flashed the grin that she loved so much. 'Not today, anyway.'

So Aladdin took his leave of the laughing princess and her confused father. At home again, he said to the genie of the lamp: 'Build me a palace of the finest marble, set with jasper, agate and other precious stones. In the middle shall be a giant hall, its four walls decked with gold and silver. Each wall is to have six windows, whose lattices must be set with thousands of diamonds, emeralds and rubies.'

'Your wish is my command,' said the genie.

The palace was finished by the next day. It was so big that it could be seen from the emperor's window, and it had velvet carpet laid all the way to his door.

'How is that possible?' the grand-vizier growled. 'It must be magic.' But the emperor did not care. His daughter was happy and so was he. He sent musicians with trumpets and cymbals to meet

Aladdin and Ching. The air rang with music and cheers all the way up to and after the wedding.

That night, the princess said goodbye to her father. Then she set out across the carpet for her new home, with her new husband and mother-in-law, Ching, at her side.

'Keep your eyes closed,' said Aladdin, as they drew nearer. Yue kept her eyes closed, and when she opened them, she gasped at the sight before her.

'It is the most beautiful thing I have ever seen!'

'Not more beautiful than you, my love.'

Ching left them kissing at the gate.

The next day Aladdin invited the emperor and his grand-vizier to see the palace. The emperor delighted in every room and counted all twenty-four jewelled windows in the hall. The grand-vizier sulked and kept muttering about magic. But like the emperor, no one cared. Everyone loved Aladdin.

As time passed, Aladdin was so generous with his fortune that the

people grew to love him even more.
It was Aladdin, not the emperor,
who gave them food when they
were hungry. It was Aladdin who
helped them when they needed
it. Thanks to him, their lives and
homes were transformed.

Far away, the sorcerer Ja'far had not forgotten about the magic lamp. He did not care about the magic *ring*, for he had already used his three wishes. But the genie of the lamp granted *unlimited* wishes. That was why he wanted it.

So when news reached Ja'far of the happy marriage of the Princess Yue to a mysterious young man with more money than the emperor, he grew suspicious.

Perhaps Aladdin had not died underground after all. Perhaps he had figured out how to summon at least one of the genies.

To find out, Ja'far travelled night and day until he reached China, and eventually Aladdin's house – but Aladdin no longer lived there. As he passed through the streets (which looked much cleaner than he remembered), Ja'far heard the people (who looked much happier than he remembered) talking about a marvellous palace.

'Forgive me,' he said, 'but what palace do you mean? The emperor's?'

'Prince Aladdin's,' they corrected him.

'*Prince* Aladdin?' Ja'far repeated.

When he saw the palace, Ja'far knew that it could only have been raised by magic. And he was furious.

'That little street rat!'

In a rage, Ja'far demanded to be let into the palace, but he was given a bag of rice and some coins instead.

'Prince Aladdin is away hunting,' they told him. 'But he hopes that this food and money will help to ease your suffering.'

After his travels, Ja'far looked so tired and dirty that the palace guards assumed he was a beggar.

They gave him what Aladdin commanded that they give to all beggars. This made Ja'far even angrier.

'I am no beggar – *he* is!'

The next time Ja'far came to the palace he was disguised as a peddler, and Aladdin was still away. The sorcerer carried a basket full of shiny copper lamps and cried 'New lamps for old! New lamps for old!' loudly as he walked. Eventually he drew quite a crowd of people watching, all of

peddler
Someone who sells goods in the street or from door to door.

whom laughed at him for such a foolish offer.

Princess Yue, sitting in the hall of twenty-four windows, sent a servant to find out what the noise was about. The servant came back laughing.

'My lady, a man is offering to exchange fine new lamps for old ones!'

Another servant, hearing this, said: 'There is an old lamp on the table that he could have.'

The lamp she meant was none

other the lamp where the genie lived. The princess, not knowing its importance, laughingly agreed that the servant should make the exchange.

This the servant did.

'Will you really give me a new lamp for this one?' she asked the sorcerer. The magic lamp was so old that no amount of polishing had ever made it look better.

Ja'far snatched it greedily. 'I will give you *all* the lamps,' he said.

Away from the palace, Ja'far waited until dark and then rubbed the lamp.

'Greetings, master,' the genie boomed. 'I am the genie of the lamp, and I will grant you–'

'Put Aladdin's palace somewhere he will never find it.'

'Your wish is my command.'

The next morning the emperor looked out of his window towards Aladdin's palace and rubbed his eyes. It was gone. He sent for the grand-vizier. He could not see it either.

'How is that possible?' said the emperor.

'I told you, Your Majesty, it must be *magic*.'

And this time the emperor cared very much, because his daughter had disappeared along with the palace.

The emperor sent men on horseback to fetch Aladdin in chains. A crowd gathered outside the emperor's palace as Aladdin was taken inside.

'Where is my daughter?' the emperor demanded.

'In the palace,' Aladdin answered, confused.

The emperor ordered the executioner to cut off Aladdin's head, thinking that this would change his answer. The executioner made Aladdin kneel down and raised his sword to strike.

'Your Majesty,' said the grand-vizier, 'wait.'

Outside the palace, all the people Aladdin had helped had begun scaling the walls to save him. They forced their way through the courtyard and looked so threatening that the emperor had no choice but to let Aladdin go.

'I do not understand!' Aladdin gasped. 'Your Majesty, what have I done to deserve this?'

'Where is my daughter?' the emperor repeated.

'In the palace!'

The emperor dragged Aladdin to his window. *And where is the palace?'*

Aladdin blinked at the empty place where his palace had been. 'How is that possible?'

'Do not pretend not to know!' the grand-vizier hissed. 'It is your own magic that has done this.'

'I do not have any magic. All I have is ...' Aladdin stopped speaking. He looked at the magic ring still on his finger. He had not used it since his mother had accidentally summoned the genie of the lamp. The ring still had one wish lift. He rubbed it then and there.

'Greetings, master,' the genie boomed. 'I–'

'Bring my palace back!'

'That is not in my power,' said the genie. 'I am only the genie of the ring; for that you must ask the genie of the lamp. I cannot undo his magic by returning the palace or the princess.'

'Then take me to my wife!'

With that, before the emperor and everyone else's shocked eyes, Aladdin vanished.

Chapter 5

It had still been daytime in China. But in the land Aladdin now found himself in, it was night. He was in the bedroom he shared with his wife, but she was not there. Aladdin crept through the shadows looking for her. 'Yue?' he whispered. *'Yue?'*

Just then something struck him on the back of the head. 'Ow!' he said loudly.

'Aladdin?'

'Yue!'

The princess put down the candlestick she had hit him with, and the couple hugged each other.

'Forgive me,' she said, 'I thought you were him!'

'Who?'

'The sorcerer!'

Aladdin paled. 'Tell me, where is the lamp that I left on the table in the hall?'

'He has it! He tricked me into giving it to him! Now he says that I must marry him. I keep saying no, but he said that you were dead. That my own father had killed you!' Yue was crying now. 'This is all my fault!' she said as Aladdin comforted her.

'It is all *my* fault,' he replied, 'for not being honest with you. If I had told you about the lamp and Ja'far none of this would have happened.'

'Who is Ja'far?'

At last, Aladdin told Yue all about himself, from his poor beginnings to the sorcerer who had accidentally led him to riches.

'What can we do?' Yue wondered.

'I do not know ...'

Just then there came a knock at the door. They had talked all night. It was morning now.

'It is the sorcerer!' Yue hissed. 'He has come to ask me to marry him again. You must go. Now.'

Aladdin left the palace through a secret passage only they knew about. As he went, an idea came to him.

To disguise himself, Aladdin exchanged clothes with the first person he came across, who spoke a language he did not know. The unfamiliar language made finding what he was looking for very difficult, but eventually he came across a town with an apothecary. To communicate what he needed to the person who worked there, he mimed being asleep. Then he was given a powder in exchange for the magic ring.

apothecary
Someone who sells or prepares medicines, now called a pharmacist. Also the name of the place where medicines are sold or prepared, now called a pharmacy.

Aladdin returned to the palace the same way he had left. 'I know what to do,' he told the princess. 'Put on your most beautiful dress and invite the sorcerer to dine with you. Let him think that you have changed your mind about marrying him.'

Yue listened carefully, and when Aladdin left her again, she dressed and sent for the sorcerer.

'I will no longer cry for my dead husband,' she told Ja'far. 'And since you tell me he was not a prince but a common street rat, my father was right to kill him. I hope you will forgive my behaviour, perhaps over some food?'

In a flash, Ja'far had summoned a feast for two.

Yue pretended to be impressed.

'And something to drink?' she suggested.

In another flash, Ja'far had summoned two cups of tea.

'How about a toast?' Yue smiled and lifted her cup. Ja'far copied her. From behind him, Aladdin tip-toed through the secret passage and added the powder to Ja'far's raised cup.

'To a new beginning,' Yue said.

'To a new beginning,' Ja'far repeated.

The princess drank deeply. So did the sorcerer.

Aladdin was creeping back towards the passageway when his borrowed shoe – which was too big for him – came off. Aladdin tripped, and Ja'far whipped around at the sound.

'You!'

The two men wrestled on the floor. With the same candlestick the princess had hit Aladdin with earlier, Yue beat against the sorcerer's back, trying to save her husband, who seemed to be losing. Ja'far was on top with his hands around Aladdin's throat. He squeezed and squeezed and squeezed – then stopped. His face turned first white, then grey, then blue. Finally, his eyes rolled back in his head and he collapsed on top of Aladdin.

'Thank goodness!' Yue gasped. 'He is finally asleep.'

But Aladdin did not think so. He rolled the sorcerer off him and checked his breathing. 'He is dead,' Aladdin said.

'From sleeping powder?' Yue questioned.

Aladdin thought back to his performance in the apothecary; how he had tried to communicate 'sleep' without words. Apparently his actions had communicated 'death' instead. He had been sold poison, *not* sleeping powder.

Aladdin had never killed anyone before, and he hoped never to do so again. But at least they were free now.

He found the magic lamp inside the sorcerer's vest and rubbed it.

'Genie, take us home.'

With that, the palace and its people were returned to China. The emperor, still mourning

mourning
The feeling and expression of great sadness that follows a death or loss.

for his lost daughter, happened to look up at his window. He rubbed his eyes. 'Grand-vizier!' he called, and the grand-vizier came.

'Am I seeing things?' the emperor demanded.

The grand-vizier was sorry to say that he was not: Aladdin was really back.

The emperor hurried to see his daughter who welcomed him warmly. She explained what had happened, and showed him the dead body of Ja'far.

'You expect us to believe that it was all the work of this sorcerer?'

the grand-vizier demanded. 'We know that your husband has a magic ring!'

'*Had* a magic ring,' the princess corrected him. 'He traded it for the poison.'

Aladdin held up his hand to show his empty finger. This was enough to convince the emperor, but not the grand-vizier.

'Your Majesty, he is lying! He still has magic or else how did he return here after the sorcerer was dead?'

This was a very good question, but by now the emperor had

begun to feel guilty about nearly having his son-in-law killed. The grand-vizier was forbidden from ever mentioning magic again, although he always knew that somehow Aladdin continued to use it, even without the ring.

Indeed, over the years, Aladdin used magic to end hunger, poverty and war. He used it to become the greatest emperor there ever was after his father-in-law died. Occasionally, he even used it to entertain his children, and then his grandchildren.

But he never again used magic for himself or his wife.

For they already had everything their hearts desired.